The Grosset Treasury of Fairy Tales

The Grosset Treasury of Fairy Tales

Pictures by Tadasu Izawa and Shigemi Hijikata

Publishers · GROSSET & DUNLAP · New York
A FILMWAYS COMPANY

Contents

Library of Congress Catalog Card Number: 76-152345
ISBN : 0-448-12290-1

Illustrations Copyright © 1967, 1968, 1969, 1971, 1977 by Tadasu Izawa and Shigemi Hijikata
through management of Dairisha, Inc. Printed and bound in Japan
by Zokeisha Publications, Ltd., Roppongi, Minato-ku, Tokyo.

Jack and The Beanstalk

Jack and his mother lived alone in a little cottage. They were so poor that they often went hungry. One day Jack's mother said that their cow would have to be sold.

As Jack led the cow to market, he met a man who said, "I will give you some magic beans for that cow." The beans looked so pretty that Jack agreed to the trade.

"Magic beans, indeed!" cried Jack's mother when he returned. "Son, how could you be so foolish!" So saying, she flung the beans out of their cottage window.

When Jack awoke next morning, he saw a tremendous beanstalk growing from the ground and reaching to the clouds. Being an adventurous lad, he began to climb it. At the top, he saw a large castle.

Jack went forward and knocked upon the door. An old woman opened it and let him in, but warned him that a wicked giant lived there.

The woman hid Jack in a closet just as the giant clumped into the room. "I smell a boy!" roared the giant. But the woman told him it was only his breakfast cooking.

After eating, the giant ordered that the magic hen be brought to him. The old woman hurried to obey. "Lay!" roared the giant — and the hen at once laid a solid gold egg.

"Now bring me my magic harp!" bellowed the giant. The old woman did so. "Play!" roared the giant — and immediately the harp played the sweetest music, all by itself.

The harp played on, and the giant's head began to nod. Soon he was asleep, snoring loudly. Jack, peeking out through a crack in the closet, had seen everything.

Jack tiptoed out of the closet, tucked the hen under one arm and the harp under the other, and ran quickly away. But the harp, being enchanted, cried out, "Master!"

The giant awoke, going after Jack, down the beanstalk. But Jack took an ax and chopped away till the beanstalk — and the giant — both fell lifeless to the ground.

From that day on, Jack and his mother, no longer poor, lived happily with the hen that laid the golden eggs and the harp that played the beautiful songs.

Cinderella

There was once a man who, having lost his wife, decided to marry again so that his gentle daughter might have a mother to care for her. But, alas, his new wife was proud and haughty, and she had two ill-tempered daughters who were not at all kind to the child. They dressed her in rags and called her Cinderella.

Now, on a certain day the King announced a great ball in honor of his son, the prince, to which all the ladies of the land were invited.

Poor Cinderella had to work harder than ever, helping her stepsisters dress for the ball.

After they had left in all their finery, Cinderella wept bitterly. "Oh, I would so like to have gone to the ball!" she cried.

At that moment her kind fairy godmother appeared.

"Hush, child," said the old lady. "You SHALL go to the ball. Fetch me a fat pumpkin, six mice, and a rat and six lizards from the garden wall."

Cinderella quickly did as she was told. Then her godmother, with a touch of her wand, turned the pumpkin into a coach drawn by six fine horses, with six tall footmen and a handsome driver.

Cinderella couldn't believe her eyes! "But I have no gown to wear," she said, looking at her ragged dress and wooden shoes.

"Tut, tut!" replied her godmother. "We'll soon fix THAT!" And she touched the girl with her wand.

Instantly Cinderella was dressed in the finest gown in the land!

"Now, off you go," said the old lady, "but you must leave the ball before the clock strikes twelve, for at that moment my magic ends, and everything will be as it was before."

Thanking her with all her heart and promising to obey, Cinderella drove off to the King's palace.

No sooner had Cinderella arrived than the prince saw her coming down the grand staircase of the ballroom. He was instantly overwhelmed by her beauty and he hastened to dance with her. The ugly stepsisters noticed her, too, but they had no

idea who the unknown lady might be, and they whispered together behind their fans. "What a beautiful gown!" said one.
"And such a lovely face!" said the other. "Now the prince won't
even look at us for the rest of the evening."

The prince refused to dance with any of the other ladies and he could scarcely take his eyes from Cinderella, so delighted was he by her charm and grace. And so the hours sped by until suddenly Cinderella heard the great clock striking the hour of midnight! With a little cry she fled from the ballroom so that the prince might not see her transformed once more into a kitchen maid. By the time she reached her carriage, she found nothing

but a large pumpkin and some mice and lizards scampering off into the night. The prince hastened after Cinderella, but she was too swift for him. As he turned sorrowfully back into the palace, what did he spy but a tiny glass slipper which Cinderella had dropped as she fled down the steps!"

"At least I have this to remind me that the lovely princess at the ball was real," said the prince sadly.

But the next day excitement spread throughout the whole kingdom. The prince had declared that the lady whose foot fitted the tiny glass slipper would become his bride.

From house to house went the royal messenger, giving everyone a chance to try on the shoe. When he arrived at the home of Cinderella, each of the ugly stepsisters tried to squeeze her foot into the tiny shoe, but to no avail.

Then Cinderella spoke up, asking to be allowed to try on the shoe. The stepsisters roared with laughter, but the messenger replied that every lady in the land was entitled to try it on. In a twinkling the glass slipper slipped neatly onto Cinderella's foot!

Then what a celebration there was! The prince was overjoyed to discover his beloved once more. The wedding was set for the next day, and never was there a more dazzling bride.

27

Cinderella, being of a kind and loving nature, gladly forgave her stepsisters for their unkind treatment of her. And, of course, she and her prince lived happily ever after.

Sleeping Beauty

Many years ago there lived a king and queen who had long wished for a child.

When at last a daughter was born to them, they were overjoyed. They named her Briar Rose and invited all the good fairies of the kingdom to come to the castle for her christening.

Each fairy in turn bestowed upon the baby princess a gift of great value. One gave her beauty, another virtue, another riches, and so on, until all but one fairy had given a gift. Just at that moment, in flew the wicked fairy who had not been invited to the christening. "How DARE you have a party without asking me?" she shrilled. Then, looking down at the little princess in her golden cradle, she cackled, "When your child is fifteen, she will prick her finger on a spindle and die!"

The king and queen were stunned, but a good fairy quickly spoke up. "I cannot undo the wicked fairy's evil spell," she said, "but my gift may soften it. The princess shall not die, but instead

will sleep for a hundred years." However, the king would not be comforted.

He ordered that all the spinning wheels in the kingdom be destroyed at once, so that his daughter could not ever prick her finger on a spindle.

And so the years passed, and Briar Rose grew up to be the loveliest princess ever seen. One day, while wandering about the courtyard of the castle, she came upon an old woman spinning. Now, of course, the princess had never seen a spinning wheel before, and when she asked the old woman, who was none other than the wicked fairy in disguise, what she was doing, the old woman cunningly showed her how to spin. Instantly Briar Rose pricked her finger on the spindle and fell down as though dead. "Ha, ha!" laughed the wicked fairy. "Now the king and queen will regret the day they did not invite me to your christening." And off she flew with her spinning wheel.

Their hearts filled with grief, the king and queen had their daughter brought to her own bedroom so that she might sleep more comfortably on her own bed.

But no sooner had this been done than a most extraordinary thing happened—everyone in the castle fell fast asleep! The cooks in the kitchen, the guards at the gates, all fell asleep right in the midst of what they were doing.

Then a briar hedge began to grow up about the castle, higher and higher, until after a number of years it was completely hidden from view. Time passed, until at last everyone in the countryside had forgotten that there had ever been a castle on that spot.

And so the years went by until it was a hundred years to the day when the princess had pricked her finger on the spindle. A handsome prince from a far country was riding through the forest when he came upon the wall of thorns. Alighting from his horse, he started to cut through the briar hedge so that he might continue on his way. No sooner did his sword touch it than the thorns drew back, making a path up to the gates of the castle!

Boldly the prince walked into the silent courtyard, and what a sight met his eyes! Everyone from the scullery maid to the king was fast asleep.

Making his way to the room where the princess slept, the prince stopped at the threshold, overwhelmed by her beauty. Then he kissed her tenderly on the lips. At that moment Briar Rose opened her eyes for the first time in a hundred years. Instantly the whole castle came back to life.

The cooks went on with their basting and tasting, the courtiers and pages paraded proudly through the courtyard, and the king and queen rejoiced to see their daughter alive once more. Briar Rose and the prince fell deeply in love with each other, and the king at once gave his consent to their marriage. Then, with the blessing of all the good fairies of the kingdom, the prince and his Sleeping Beauty lived happily together for the rest of their lives.

The Elves and the Shoemaker

There was once an honest shoemaker who had become so poor that he had enough leather for only one pair of shoes. He cut these out, and because it was late by then, he lay down and fell asleep.

In the morning, when he came to his work table, he was surprised to find that the pair of shoes he had cut was standing on the table, finished to the last seam.

He examined the shoes carefully. The work was neat and not a stitch was out of place. Clearly an expert had worked on them.

A short time later a customer came in. She was so happy with the shoes, she paid more than the usual price. Now the shoemaker was able to buy enough leather for two pairs of shoes. That evening he cut them out and went to bed.

He woke up the next morning all ready to go to work, but there were the two pairs of shoes finished as expertly as before! Customers came for them, and now the shoemaker had money to buy leather for four pairs of shoes. Again he cut the leather in the evening, and in the morning all were expertly finished.

This went on day after day, so that before long the shoemaker became a wealthy man.

One evening he said to his wife, "Let us stay up tonight to see who has been helping us all this time." His wife agreed and they lit a candle on the table, then hid in a corner behind the shoemaker's work clothes. Imagine their surprise when at midnight two tiny men dressed in ragged clothes came in and began stitching, sewing and hammering!

The shoes were finished before dawn. Then the tiny men ran off.

The next day the wife said, "The little men have been so good to us that we should do something for them. They must be cold in their raggedy clothes... I will sew them some shirts, coats and trousers, and knit them sweaters and stockings."

"And I will make them shoes," added the husband.

A few days later all the new clothes were
finished, and then, instead of the cut leather,
the shoemaker and his wife laid them out on
the work table.

When the two little men came in, they were so surprised and delighted with their lovely new clothes that they hopped and danced all over the room. Then they skipped out the door and down the street. The shoemaker never saw them again.

From that time on, the shoemaker prospered in everything he did, and he and his wife lived happily for the rest of their days.

Little Red Riding Hood

Many years ago there lived a little girl who, whenever she went out, wore a cape and hood of bright red wool. For this reason she was called Little Red Riding Hood.

One day her grandmother, who lived in a house on the other side of the woods, became ill. Little Red Riding Hood's mother asked her if she would carry a basket of goodies to her, but she warned her daughter not to speak to anyone she might meet on the way.

Off through the green woods went the little girl, singing a happy song to herself as she skipped along.

She had not gone very far when she met a wolf with very bright eyes. "Good day, my little maid," he said, bowing politely. His long red tongue hung out as he thought of what a juicy tidbit she would make for his supper. "And where are you going this lovely spring morning?" he asked.

Little Red Riding Hood, who had forgotten all about her mother's advice, explained that she was on her way to visit her sick grandmother on the other side of the woods. She saw some bright flowers and stopped to pick a few to put in her basket.

When she looked up, the wolf was running into the woods as fast as he could go, his coattails flying behind him. He had thought of a way to make a meal of both Little Red Riding Hood and her grandmother!

Meanwhile, in the cottage on the other side of the woods, Little Red Riding Hood's grandmother in her shawl and nightcap looked out of the window from her bed, wondering if her beloved grandchild would come to visit her that day. She thought she caught a glimpse of her red hood far down the forest path.

Suddenly into the cottage burst the wolf, who had taken a shortcut through the woods. Overturning a chair, he pounced upon the startled old lady, quickly bundled her into a cupboard, and locked the door.

"Now to make ready for Red Riding Hood's visit," he said to
himself with a grin. "It will take only a minute."

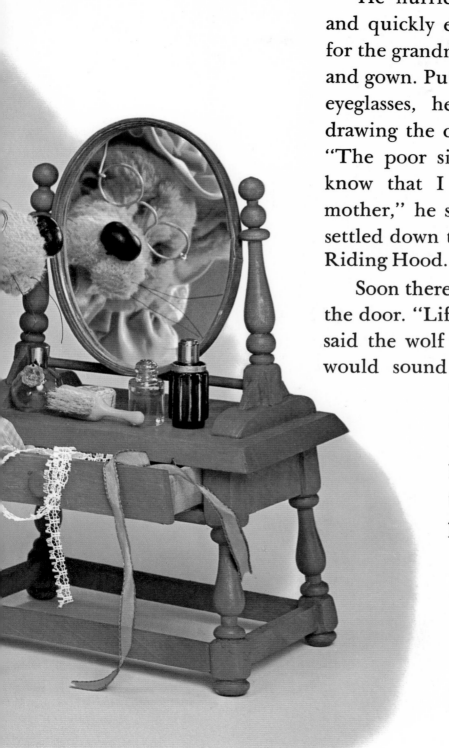

He hurried into the bedroom and quickly exchanged his clothes for the grandmother's lace nightcap and gown. Putting on the old lady's eyeglasses, he jumped into bed, drawing the covers up to his chin. "The poor simple girl will never know that I am not her grandmother," he said to himself, as he settled down to wait for Little Red Riding Hood.

Soon there was a gentle knock at the door. "Lift the latch, my dear," said the wolf in a voice he hoped would sound like a trembly old lady's. "You'll find me in the bedroom."

In came Little Red Riding Hood with the bouquet she had picked in the woods.

"Grandmother," she cried, "what big eyes you have!"

"All the better to see you with," said the wolf slyly.

"Grandmother," added the girl, "what big ears you have!"

"All the better to hear you with, my child," said the wolf, licking his lips greedily.

By now Little Red Riding Hood was feeling a bit frightened. Her grandmother had never looked so strange before! Then she said, "But, Grandmother, what big teeth you have!" And at that, the wolf jumped out of bed, upsetting the table in his hurry.

"All the better to eat you with!" he shouted, and began chasing Little Red Riding Hood, who cried, "Help! Help!"

Fortunately, Little Red Riding Hood's father happened to be hunting in the woods nearby and, hearing her cry for help, he hurried toward the house. There he wasted not a minute in shooting the wolf and comforting his frightened child.

"But what has happened to Grandmother?" asked Little Red Riding Hood as she dried her tears. "Do you suppose the wolf has eaten her up?"

Just then they heard a great thumping in the cupboard, and when the door was opened, out tumbled the old lady, safe and sound.

You may be sure that never again did Little Red Riding Hood speak to a wolf in the woods!

Hansel and Gretel

In a humble cottage in a forest there lived a poor woodchopper with his wife and two children, Hansel and Gretel. There wasn't much to eat, even in good times, but at last the day came when there was no food at all.

That night, after the children had gone to bed, the woodchopper said, "What will become of us? How can we live without food?"

His wife, who had an unkind heart, replied, "Tomorrow we'll take the children into the deepest woods, and leave them. Then we will have only two mouths to feed."

Now, the children, who had been too hungry to sleep, heard this, and Gretel began to cry. "Dear Hansel," she moaned, "what shall we do?"

Hansel tried to comfort his sister. "Don't be afraid," he said. "I have a plan that will help us to find our way back home."

Early the next morning the children were awakened. "Come," said the mother, "we must all go into the woods to find food." Hansel brought along a crust of stale bread that he had found and dropped tiny crumbs along the path so that they could find their way home again.

When they reached the deepest part of the forest, the mother told the children to lie down to rest. While Hansel and Gretel dozed in the warm sunlight, she and her husband slipped back through the forest to the cottage.

The tired, hungry children were soon fast asleep. When night came, their guardian angels hovered over them to keep them from harm.

In the morning, when they awoke, Hansel went to look for the trail of bread crumbs. Alas! the forest birds had eaten every one. So Hansel and Gretel wandered this way and that through the woods, looking for berries to eat.

Suddenly, ahead of them in a clearing, they saw a house made of gingerbread and cakes and candies! Joyfully they rushed up to the house and began to eat whatever they could break off.

At that moment an old woman appeared. She smiled sweetly and invited Hansel and Gretel into her house for a proper meal. What delicious food they had to eat! The children ate until they could hold no more. Then the woman tucked them tenderly into bed for the night.

Now, it so happened that this old woman was a crafty old witch, and she planned to fatten Hansel and Gretel in order to eat them. The next morning she awakened the children with a rough shake, and dragged Hansel off to a cage and locked him up. She made Gretel do all the housework and cooking.

Poor Gretel cried and cried, but it was no use. Each day the best food she cooked was served to Hansel, because the old witch wanted him nice and plump before she ate him.

The children soon noticed that the old witch could not see very well. Each time she came to Hansel's cage, she demanded to feel his finger so that she could tell how fat he was getting. And each time Hansel would hold out a skinny little bone. The witch would go away, saying, "I'll wait a few more days. He is still much too thin."

But at last she could wait no longer. She ordered Gretel to make the fire good and hot so that she could prepare her feast.

With a sad heart the little girl started a hot fire in the oven. Soon the witch bustled into the kitchen, asking how the fire was coming along.

"I cannot tell," answered Gretel. "I have never made such a large fire before."

"Out of my way, foolish girl!" said the impatient witch. "I will see for myself."

As she opened the door and leaned forward to look, Gretel gave the wicked witch a tremendous push. Into the fire she tumbled! Gretel quickly shut the heavy door and ran to free her brother.

What a time they had going through the witch's house! Chests of jewels and bags of gold were everywhere! After stuffing their pockets with all they would hold, the children fled forever from the house of the wicked witch.

They presently came to a lake, and seeing no way to cross, the children gave up hope of ever getting home. But soon a white swan appeared, and offered to carry them across the lake on his back. When they arrived on the other shore, who should be there cutting wood but their father! He was overjoyed to see his beloved children again, and the children lost no time in showing him their treasures.

After thanking the swan for his help, Hansel and Gretel and the woodchopper returned to live happily once more in their cottage in the woods.

Snow White

and the
Seven Dwarfs

There was once a wicked queen who had a magic mirror. Each day she would ask it, "Who is fairest in the land?" The mirror each time would answer, "You are, oh queen."

But as time passed, the queen's own stepchild, Snow White, grew up, becoming more beautiful. One day the magic mirror told the queen, "Snow White is fairer, by far."

In a fit of rage, the queen ordered a huntsman to take Snow White into the deep forest and kill her at once. Seizing the girl, the huntsman led Snow White away.

But in the woods he took pity on her and said, "Run away, poor child!" So Snow White ran and ran until she came upon a little house. She went into it to rest.

This was the house of the seven dwarfs. When the little men came home, Snow White told them her sad story. The kind dwarfs agreed that she should stay with them.

During the day, Snow White kept house while the dwarfs went to work at their mine. To keep her from harm, the little men warned her never to let anyone into the house.

Learning from the magic mirror that Snow White still lived, the queen prepared a poisoned apple. Then, disguised as a beggar woman, she went to the house in the woods.

Snow White answered the knock at the door, but would not let the beggar woman in. "Then at least have a bite of this apple, my dear," cackled the woman.

So rosy red was the apple that Snow White could not resist. But after only one bite, the beautiful girl fell to the ground. The queen, laughing loudly, then dashed away.

When the dwarfs found Snow White, they could not rouse her. Sorrowfully they placed her in a glass case, so that they could gaze upon her beauty always.

One day a handsome prince happened by, and seeing the lovely girl, kissed her. At that, Snow White awakened. The prince loved her dearly.